THE SKY'S THE LIMIT

ASK FOR HELP

BY SUSANNE M. BUSHMAN

BLUE OWL BOOKS

TIPS FOR CAREGIVERS

Social and emotional learning (SEL) helps children manage emotions, learn how to feel empathy, create and achieve goals, and make good decisions. Strong lessons and support in SEL will help children establish positive habits in communication, cooperation, and decision-making. By incorporating SEL in early reading, children will be better equipped to build confidence and foster positive peer networks.

BEFORE READING

Talk to the reader about asking for help. Explain that asking for help is healthy.

Discuss: Does everyone ask for help sometimes? When have you asked for help? How did it feel? Were you glad that you asked for help?

AFTER READING

Talk to the reader about different people they can ask for help.

Discuss: Who around you can you ask for help? How can you decide who is the best person to help you? What should you do after someone helps you? What could you help someone else with?

SEL GOAL

Some children may be nervous or embarrassed to ask for help. They may feel ashamed or as if they have failed because they cannot do something by themselves. They may worry that others are judging them because they need help. They could worry that they are bothering those around them by asking for help. Help readers understand that it's OK to ask for help. Brainstorm a list of people they have seen ask for help.

TABLE OF CONTENTS

CHAPTER 1
Everyone Needs Help … 4

CHAPTER 2
People Who Help … 8

CHAPTER 3
Helping Others … 18

GOALS AND TOOLS
Grow with Goals … 22
Writing Reflection … 22
Glossary … 23
To Learn More … 23
Index … 24

CHAPTER 1

EVERYONE NEEDS HELP

You can do many things all by yourself! Maybe you can climb a tree or read your favorite book without help.

But sometimes you will need help. This could be when you are learning a new skill, like playing piano. Or maybe you need help to **improve** skills you already have, like reading. You might need help overcoming a **challenge**, like starting at a new school.

The people in your life are there to **support** you. But sometimes they can't see that you need help. So you may have to ask for it!

Asking for help can be hard. You want to be able to do things alone. But when you've tried and can't do something yourself, asking for help is healthy. When you ask for help, you build a **network**. Who is in it? It is made of people you trust!

TRY TO HELP YOURSELF

When you have a problem, first ask if you can help yourself. Think of ways that you can help you! If that doesn't work, don't wait to ask someone you trust for help. Some problems get bigger over time.

CHAPTER 2

PEOPLE WHO HELP

Maybe you don't know how to ride a bike. Most of your friends already know how. You feel **embarrassed**. Remember! Everyone had to learn at one point. When you ask, your dad is happy to teach you!

We don't understand every lesson right away. This might make you feel **ashamed**. But your teacher is there to help you learn. He can answer your questions!

Do you struggle with your favorite sport? This is OK! Everyone has different strengths. Your friend is really good. You can ask her for tips. Tell her you noticed her skills. It is nice to **compliment** others. Then she understands why you are asking for her help.

WE ALL NEED HELP

You might think you are the only one who needs help. You are not! We all face challenges in one way or another. We can all help each other!

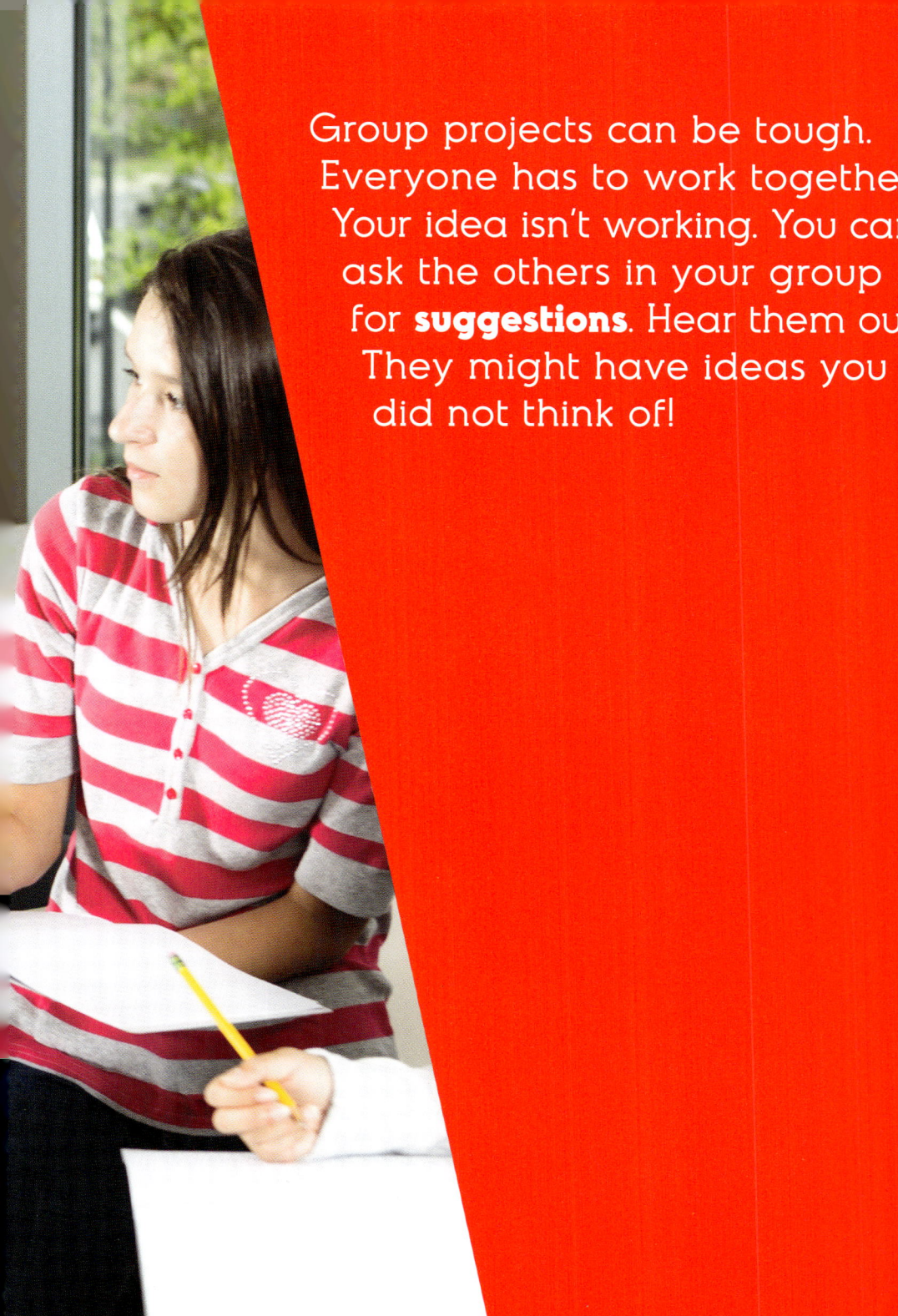

Group projects can be tough. Everyone has to work together. Your idea isn't working. You can ask the others in your group for **suggestions**. Hear them out. They might have ideas you did not think of!

CHAPTER 2

Maybe you are being bullied. You ask your friend for **advice**. Why? She has dealt with bullies before. She tells you to ignore their mean words.

Trusted adults can help, too! Like who? The school **counselor**, principal, and teachers are all there to help. They can give you advice. They can talk to the bullies.

TELL SOMEONE

Maybe your problem isn't getting better. Tell someone about it. Nothing is too bad to tell someone about. Find a trusted adult to help you.

We all have bad days sometimes. You try drawing a picture. This usually makes you feel better. But you still feel sad. It's OK! What else could you do? Call a friend! He can listen to your feelings and help cheer you up!

Be sure to thank your friend. Let him know that you **appreciate** him!

CHAPTER 2 17

CHAPTER 3
HELPING OTHERS

Your network supports you. You can support them, too! Your grandma may ask for help doing chores. It's nice to help! Helping shows you care.

Be sure to ask if you can help! Does someone you know use a wheelchair? Ask if you can open the door. It is OK if someone doesn't want help. It is still nice to ask!

Some people don't like to ask for help. Your brother doesn't say it, but you can tell he is struggling with math. You are good at math. You can offer to help. Let him know you are there.

When we help each other, we show we care. How do you help others?

CHAPTER 3   21

GOALS AND TOOLS

GROW WITH GOALS

Everyone needs help sometimes. Even adults need help. We can get better at asking for help and being thankful for it.

Goal: Help others who may need help! You might have a friend who needs help learning something you already know. Teach him or her what you know. You might learn something new in the process, too!

Goal: Identify people who support you. Think about the people in your life. Who are good people to ask for help? What are the best things to ask them to help with?

Goal: Identify your strengths and weaknesses. What are things that you don't need help with? What are things that you could ask for help to improve on?

WRITING REFLECTION

Reflecting on times you successfully asked for help can make you more comfortable asking for help in the future.

1. When did you last ask for help?
2. Write about who you asked and what improved because you asked for help.
3. When are other good times to ask for help?

GLOSSARY

advice
A suggestion about what someone should do.

appreciate
To enjoy or value somebody or something.

ashamed
Feeling embarrassed or guilty.

challenge
Something that is difficult and requires extra effort or work to do.

compliment
To make a remark or do something to show admiration or appreciation.

counselor
Someone trained to help with problems or give advice.

embarrassed
To be ashamed and uncomfortable.

improve
To get better or to make better.

network
An interconnected group of people.

suggestions
Things that are mentioned as ideas, plans, or possibilities.

support
To give help, comfort, or encouragement to someone or something.

TO LEARN MORE

Finding more information is as easy as 1, 2, 3.

1. Go to www.factsurfer.com
2. Enter "**askforhelp**" into the search box.
3. Choose your cover to see a list of websites.

INDEX

advice 14

alone 7

appreciate 17

ashamed 9

bike 8

bullied 14

challenge 5, 10

chores 18

compliment 10

counselor 14

embarrassed 8

friends 8, 10, 14, 17

improve 5

network 7, 18

principal 14

questions 9

read 4, 5

school 5, 14

skill 5, 10

suggestions 13

support 7, 18

teacher 9, 14

Blue Owl Books are published by Jump!, 5357 Penn Avenue South, Minneapolis, MN 55419, www.jumplibrary.com

Copyright © 2020 Jump! International copyright reserved in all countries. No part of this book may be reproduced in any form without written permission from the publisher.

Library of Congress Cataloging-in-Publication Data is available at www.loc.gov or upon request from the publisher.

ISBN: 978-1-64527-196-3 (hardcover)
ISBN: 978-1-64527-197-0 (paperback)
ISBN: 978-1-64527-198-7 (ebook)

Editor: Jenna Trnka
Designer: Molly Ballanger

Photo Credits: Sergiy Bykhunenko/Shutterstock, cover; kali9/iStock, 1, 12–13; Sean Locke Photography/Shutterstock, 3; ArrowStudio/Shutterstock, 4; Image Source/iStock, 5; Rock and Wasp/Shutterstock, 6–7; michaejung/Shutterstock, 8; FatCamera/iStock, 9; miodrag ignjatovic/iStock, 10–11; Steve Debenport/iStock, 14–15; monkeybusinessimages/iStock, 16–17; Mahathir Mohd Yasin/Shutterstock, 18; Daisy-Daisy/iStock, 19; Zuraisham Salleh/iStock, 20–21; Nic Keller/Shutterstock, 23.

Printed in the United States of America at Corporate Graphics in North Mankato, Minnesota.